WITHDRAWN

Before We Sleep
This edition published in 2021 by Red Comet Press, LLC, Brooklyn, NY

First published as *Prima di dormire*
Original Italian text © 2019 Giorgio Volpe
Illustrations © 2019 Paolo Proietti
Published by arrangement with Kite edizioni S.r.l.
English translation © 2021 Red Comet Press, LLC
Adapted and translated by Angus Yuen-Killick

Library of Congress Control Number: 2020948895
ISBN: 978-1-63655-004-6

20 21 22 23 24 25 TLF 10 9 8 7 6 5 4 3 2 1

Manufactured in China

RED COMET PRESS

RedCometPress.com

Before We Sleep

Giorgio Volpe & Paolo Proietti

Red Comet Press • Brooklyn

As the season turned, the forest was dressed in new colors of rich amber, burned orange, and chestnut brown.

Little Red the fox was happy, because now it would be much easier to hide.

A fox would be hard to spy among the dried brown leaves, burgundy bushes, and coppery grasses. Only in the open meadow would Hazel the dormouse be able to catch sight of Little Red.

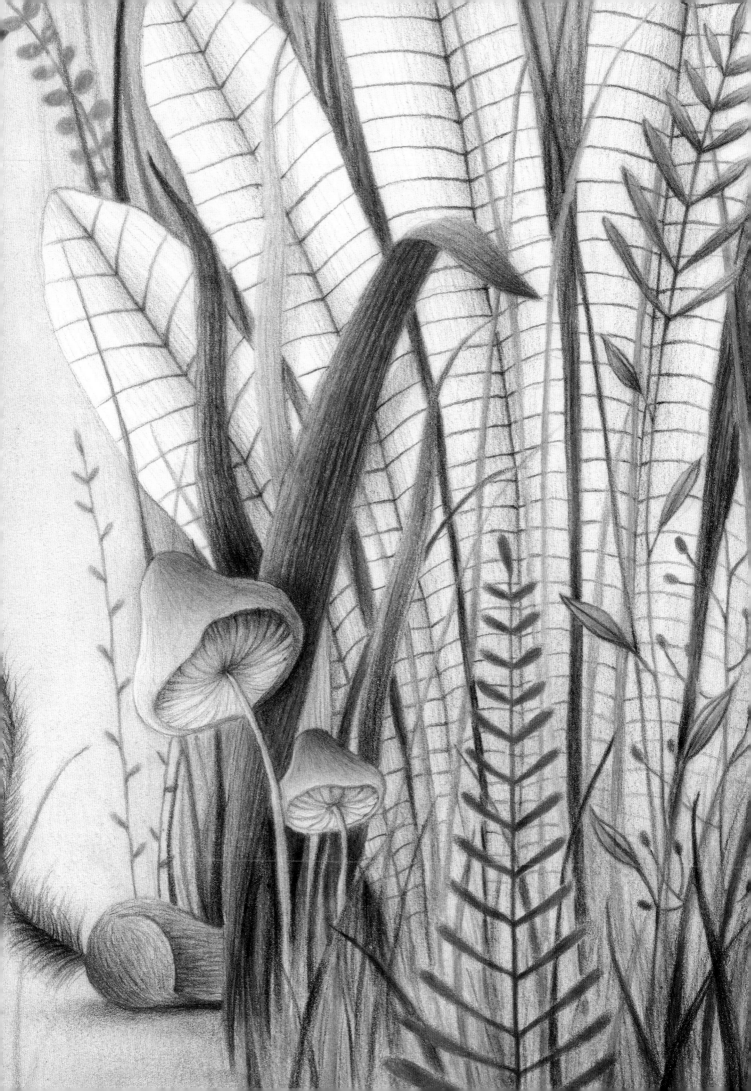

Little Red and Hazel spent hours and hours playing hide-and-seek together.

The two friends loved jumping and rolling in the crisp dried leaves.

They loved the rustling sound. "The leaves are laughing with us," said Hazel joyfully.

During these moments of happiness,
the cold air hinted of the coming winter.
Little Red felt a tinge of sadness.
For Red, the smell of winter meant
one thing: loneliness.

Soon, Little Red's very best friend
in the world would settle down in
a warm burrow to hibernate.

"Hazel, perhaps this season, you will sleep less,"
said Little Red hopefully, trying to sound cheerful.

"Little Red, I am no fox,
    I am a dormouse. I'd like to stay
    awake and keep you company,
    but you know, in the end,
    I must always sleep."

So Little Red started to think of ways
to keep Hazel from falling asleep.

What if I could make the sun stay high?
Then winter would not be so cold.

What if I could ask the forest to hold its fruit?
Then there would be food all winter long.

What if I tickled Hazel to stay awake?
Then we could play and play.

The dormouse started to yawn.

"Hazel, I want us to stay together forever,"
pleaded the friend.

"Little Red, I promise, when the winter
gives way to spring, I will be here for you,
and we will play again."

"I know, Hazel, but before you sleep,
may I tell you a story?"

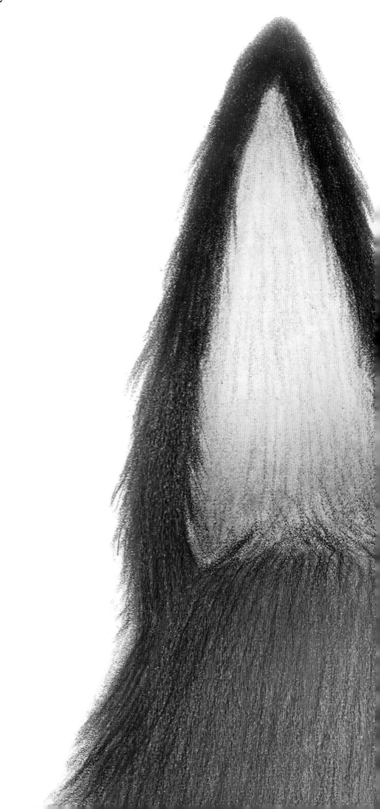

"Why . . . yes, ahh . . . as long as it
is short," replied Hazel sleepily,
with head nodding and eyes closing.

So Little Red curled up on the forest floor
and Hazel nestled into the soft warm tail to listen.

But, before a word of the story was spoken . . .
the two friends had fallen fast asleep, together.